HAUNTIQUES

Hauntiques
is published by Stone Arch Books,
a Capstone imprint
1710 Roe Crest Drive
North Mankato, Minnesota 56003
www.mycapstone.com

Cataloging-in-Publication Data is available on
the Library of Congress website.
ISBN: 978-1-4965-3548-1 (reinforced library bound)
ISBN: 978-1-4965-3552-8 (eBook pdf)

Summary:
When a spooky antique doll begins playing tricks on its new owner,
the Hauntique Hunters of Two Mile Creek find out that a local
woman used to make dolls by at the Darling Doll company. From
there, they gather clues to bring the mystery to light.

Photo Credits: Nathan Lewis, author photo

Designer: Hilary Wacholz

Printed in Canada.
009636F16

HAUNTIQUES

DARLING DOLL

written by Thomas Kingsley Troupe

illustrated by Rudy Faber

STONE ARCH BOOKS
a capstone imprint

Hai and I stand outside our school's side entrance. "Casey, you have to go to the dance! You can't turn around and go back home now."

With caution, I eye the familiar brick building where I attend sixth grade. "I don't know," I say. "I really don't feel so good."

Hai groans. "That feeling in your stomach?" Hai says, pointing at my gut. "That's nerves. Think of all the spooky stuff we've seen lately. And *this* is what's going to finally scare you?"

He's right.

Ever since the Markles moved to our small town of Two Mile Creek and opened the Days Gone Buy antique store, we've gotten tangled up in a number of paranormal misadventures. In the last two months, I've seen stuff that would scare the pants off of most people. We've encountered a haunted hockey puck, a possessed record player that only played one song, and a creepy wagon that rolled through our neighborhood all on its own.

Sounds random, right? Well, Days Gone Buy used to be Red's General Store, a place that was closed up for decades. When the Markles bought it and fixed it up, they acquired a basement full of antiques that old Red himself used to collect. So far, three things they've sold from Red's collection have had ghosts attached.

Somehow, we got roped into helping Liz and Beth, the twin Markle daughters, figure out how to help the ghosts move on.

Sure, Hai and I are good guys. But to tell the whole story, Beth Markle is also partly why I'm standing in the parking lot right now. I've been having second thoughts about going to our first middle school dance. They're calling it the Spring Fever Dance, but I think I've got a fever of my own.

I like Beth. A lot. And I slipped up and told her so just recently. She was nice enough to say she liked me, too. But who knows? Maybe she just likes me as a friend or something. But she *did* hug me.

"Casey?" Hai asks, catching me totally zoning out. "You still there? You look like you've been plugged with a tranquilizer dart."

"I'm fine," I say, shaking it off.

"Good," Hai says. He grabs the sleeve of my jacket and begins tugging at me. "Then let's get inside."

"I still don't know," I say.

"You like Beth," Hai says. "Beth likes you. You said so yourself. What don't you know?"

I'm about to tell him I'm heading back home to spend the night staring at the wall when I hear a familiar voice.

"Hey, Willis! Hey, Boon!"

John Muffleman and a couple of other guys from our class strut up the sidewalk. They're dressed like they're headed for a dance that's much fancier than advertised. Muffleman even has a tie on.

Last week, I found out John Muffleman likes Beth, too. Muffleman's popular and a nice enough guy, and other than liking the girl I've got my eye on, I really have no problem with him. But imagining Beth as his girlfriend makes my stomach even twistier than it is now.

"Hey, Muffleman," Hai says. "Prom isn't for another couple of years, man."

"Ha-ha," Muffleman says. "We just want to look good for the ladies."

A minute ago, I wanted to go home. Now, I want to get inside — fast.

"Good to see you guys," I say. I nod at Hai. "We should probably get in there."

Hai blinks a few times as if he's trying to figure me out and then smiles. "Yeah," he says. "Let's do this, Willis."

I don't think they spent a whole lot of time decorating the cafeteria for the Spring Fever Dance. Music with lots of keyboards, the kind only people my parents' age listen to, plays through two speakers on either side of the room. Mr. Harper, our free-spirited music and art teacher by day and our DJ for the night, has set up his laptop. A tiny disco ball throws pinpricks of light that pattern the dance floor and illuminate a couple of handmade signs that have been taped up. I notice that one of them is misspelled: *SPIRNG FEVER*.

My eyes follow the spinning lights to the wall, where almost all of the boys are standing. The girls line the wall on the opposite side of the room. A few adventurous guys are out dancing to some song that sounds like a mix of yodeling, sci-fi sound effects, and a drum machine from the 1980s.

A small cluster of girls also huddles out on the dance floor. The only body parts moving are their mouths. They're probably gossiping.

"Where's your girl, Casey?" Hai asks.

"I'm not sure," I say, my stomach bubbling and churning. I'm watching the doorway anytime anyone walks past it.

Mr. Harper plays two more songs from bands who've likely broken up decades ago before firing up a slow love song. Immediately, the dance floor completely empties.

"Too bad Beth's not around," Hai says. "This would be the song."

At the doorway, two nearly identical shadows come in from the bright hallway. My heart shifts to fifth gear as Liz and Beth Markle enter the cafeteria.

"Dude," Hai whispers, elbowing my ribs.

"Oh," I say, finding it hard to catch my breath. "Cool."

The Markle twins pause for a second as Liz surveys the room. When she sees the wall where all of the other girls are standing, she drags Beth over. I watch as Beth checks out the rest of the place. Maybe she's looking for me?

"Don't be shy," Mr. Harper says. "Get on out and dance, people!" Usually, his voice sounds nasally, but tonight he purrs like a radio guy. "Those walls don't need you to hold 'em up!"

A few people actually head for the floor. I watch Ryan Preston ask Holly Webber to dance. Nick Comstock walks over and gets Sarah Richie off the wall. I can see both Beth and Liz are waiting.

"Do it," Hai whispers. "This is your chance, man."

"I don't know," I say. "I might embarrass her or scare her off."

And now Liz is walking across the cafeteria. At first, I think she's coming over to us. Instead, she gives us the stink eye before marching over to where big Joe Stewell is standing, a few feet to my right.

"Let's go, Joe," Liz says. Joe makes a face like he was dropped in the middle of nowhere. Grabbing him by the arm, Liz tugs Joe onto the dance floor.

The six or seven dancing couples on the floor look a bit uncomfortable. None of them appears to be talking to each other.

They sway back and forth, their hands clamped onto their partners' shoulders and waists as the song's lead singer belts out the soulful refrain.

And now Muffleman steps away from the wall.

"Uh-oh," Hai whispers.

I'm done standing against the wall. I'm making a beeline for Beth Markle and dodging the dancing couples on the floor. I have to reach Beth before Muffleman.

My throat is all tight and twitchy as I slip past Ryan and Holly. Along the wall, Beth is watching her shoes. The space where her sister was standing is empty.

I'm thinking fast, wondering what I'll say. *Hey Beth, it's me, Casey. Remember?* No. That sounds dumb. *Let's dance, Beth. This could be the song we remember when we're old.* Whoa. Too much.

Muffleman is closing in. There's no time to screw around. Two more steps and —

"Hey," I say, standing in front of Beth. "Hi. Hello, Beth."

Beth looks up at me and pokes her glasses in place with one quick move. Even in the mostly dark of the cafeteria, her blue eyes sparkle. Her smile makes me forget where I am for a second.

"Casey," she says. "Hi."

"So," I say. "Yeah. I thought maybe you might want . . . " Suddenly, I can't remember what I was thinking. *Something she might want? A puppy? A firm handshake? A year's supply of gum?*

"To dance?" Beth says as if offering to help. She knows I'm shy, and she is, too. One of the reasons why we're perfect for each other.

"Yeah," I say. "I'd love to. I mean, we should."

Just as I say that, the music stops. In the space of two seconds, I go from being triumphant to crushed.

"The song is over," Beth says, sounding as disappointed as I feel. "But maybe . . ."

Suddenly, Mr. Harper, my new favorite teacher of all time, fires up another slow song.

"It just started," I say. I lead her out onto the dance floor, and my face splits into a smile. I watch poor John Muffleman slink back to the wall. He glances over at me with a dejected smirk on his face.

When we find a spot in the crowd, we arrange our hands, mine at her waist and hers on my shoulders. I look at her, and she's looking back at me. We both smile before checking out everyone else. Liz sees the two of us and shakes her head. When she and Joe turn around, Joe gives me the thumbs up.

"Is this your first dance?" Beth asks.

"Yeah," I say. "Sorry if I'm lousy at it. I don't really dance a lot."

"You're doing fine," Beth says. "We had one at my old school right before we moved here."

"Oh, cool," I say and wonder if she had a serious boyfriend she had to leave behind. Maybe this whole dance is bumming her out.

"I just stood there the whole night," Beth says. "I feared the same would happen tonight."

"I almost didn't come inside," I say. "I got really nervous or whatever."

"Really?" Beth says. "What were you so nervous about?"

"Well," I say, my shoulders tingling from Beth's touch, "I was nervous about asking you to dance."

Beth is quiet for a second. I'm guessing I've totally creeped her out.

"I'm glad you did," she says.

After the dance, I'm walking home with Hai. He's going to stay overnight to play video games. I don't even care that he'll probably destroy me in any game we play, because I've just had the best night ever. It's weird to think I almost skipped the whole thing because I was feeling chicken.

I'm so proud of myself, I want to do a back flip right here on the sidewalk.

"So did you kiss her?" Hai says.

"No," I say. "Not yet. But some people were asking me if we were boyfriend and girlfriend."

"What'd you say?"

"I just shrugged and said I didn't know," I say.

"Good call," Hai says. "Muffleman was seriously bummed. He even took his tie off halfway through the night."

"Yeah," I say. "I feel just awful about that, but I guess I'll get over it."

"Ha," Hai says. "Nice. Crazy about Liz and Joe getting together, isn't it?"

"Yeah," I say. "Who knew?"

When we get to my house, I glance up and stop dead in my tracks. Hai takes a couple more steps and stops, too. He glances back at me.

"You okay, Casey?"

"Who. Is. That?" I say. I point up at the upper window of my next-door neighbor's house.

Hai follows my finger. In a matter of seconds, we're both staring up at the window. Standing between the curtains is a girl. Dark hair frames a ghostly white girl's face. Shadows make her eyes black and empty as if they don't have eyeballs anymore. Maybe it's the moonlight.

Hai scratches his head and asks, "Does your neighbor have a kid?"

"She doesn't have any kids," I say.

I watch the girl in the window, but she doesn't move or blink. She's just staring off somewhere else. That's when it hits me.

"I think it's a doll or something," I whisper.

"Whoa, that's a creepy doll," Hai says.

"Totally," I say. "I wonder why she's staring out the window."

"To freak us out?" Hai replies.

I can't stop staring at the doll and her blank face. It seems as though she'll turn and gaze down at us from up on the second floor. I know Mrs. LaPierre, the lady who lives there, but she isn't someone who would pose a doll like that just to be funny. I also know she doesn't have any kids. It gives me an uneasy feeling.

"Maybe I'll just go back to my house and sleep," Hai says. "I don't like knowing there's a possessed doll staring out from a window nearby."

"Dude," I say trying to sound brave, "it's just a doll." I hold back a shudder. "Either way," I say, "you're not leaving me alone tonight."

Hai shakes his head, and we head inside. I fire up the oven, toss a frozen pizza in, and we take up game controllers. By the time Hai hits his second grand slam in the third inning of *Baseball Heroes 5: Touch 'Em All!,* I've forgotten all about the doll.

Instead, I think about dancing with Beth.

Hai loves video games. When I wake up on the couch Saturday morning, I look over to the love seat where Hai's still asleep, game controller still in hand. I laugh, get up, and head to the kitchen.

My dad's in there pulling out a skillet. "You guys have fun last night?" he asks. He sets the skillet down on the counter and fishes around for the plug that goes in the side.

"Yeah," I said. "A lot of fun."

Mom swoops in. "Dance with any girls?" she asks, raising her eyebrows as she sips her cup of coffee.

"I might have," I admit.

"Oh," Mom says. "Who, who?"

"You sound like an owl, Mom," I say, trying not to make eye contact.

"Come on, Case," Dad says. He fits the metal spike into the skillet and plugs it into the wall. "If you end up marrying this girl, we'll find out eventually."

"Maybe you danced with all the girls?" Mom asks. "You heartbreaker, you."

Dad smiles at Mom's comment.

"I danced with Beth Markle," I say proudly. "The girl whose parents own Days Gone Buy."

"Right, yeah," Dad says. "The old junk shop. Well, that's great news considering you didn't even want to go last night."

"I know," I say. "But I'm glad I did."

"Are you two *boyfriend-girlfriend* now?" Mom asks. I realize then how many times in the last twelve hours or so I've been asked that question. Maybe my classmates and adults aren't that different.

"I don't know," I say. "Not sure how that works officially."

Out the kitchen window, I see Mrs. LaPierre's car parked in her driveway. I turn and peer up to where Hai and I spotted the creepy doll last night.

It's no longer there.

"Well, look who's awake," Dad says.

I turn and see a sleepy-eyed Hai shuffle into the kitchen.

"Wow," I say. "You look like a zombie."

"Well, we're fresh out of brains, Hai," Mom says. "But maybe some eggs and bacon?"

"Bacon?" Hai says. "I'd love some bacon."

We eat our breakfast. Mom and Dad do their best to pump us for more information about the dance, but we're not giving in. As we help with the dishes, there's a knock on our front door.

My mom wipes her hands on the dish towel and answers the door.

"Casey," Mom says in a goofy sing-song voice. "It's for yooooou . . . "

I zip over to the front door, Hai following.

Beth Markle stands in the entryway. "Hi, Casey," she says. "Hi, Hai."

We greet her back, but from Beth's look, I realize that my face can't hide my confusion.

"How well do you know your neighbor, Casey?" she asks.

It doesn't take a rocket scientist to know what this is about. "It's the doll, isn't it?" I ask.

◆

On the way next door, Beth lets us know that Mrs. LaPierre called the store before they were even open. She asked Beth if she or her family had noticed anything strange about the doll before they sold it to her. Instead of letting her parents know about yet another potentially haunted antique, she told Mrs. LaPierre she'd come and take a look.

I've known Mrs. LaPierre all my life. She's been our neighbor since long before I was born. She's kind of quiet, works at the insurance office in town, and is pretty much an all-around nice lady.

I've never been inside her house, but today, Hai, Beth, and I sit on a couch in her living room. I can see she's rather frazzled.

"I don't know what's going on," Mrs. LaPierre says. "I came home this morning and found the doll standing in the window."

"We saw that last night," Hai said. "Casey and me, I mean."

"You did?" Mrs. LaPierre says. "What time?"

"Sometime after ten or so," I say.

"You didn't see anything out of place around the house?" she asks. "A prowler, perhaps?"

"No," I say. "I just noticed the doll in the window. I thought it was a real girl at first."

Mrs. LaPierre seems afraid. I guess I would be freaked, too, if I were her.

"There wasn't any sign of a break-in, nothing stolen," Mrs. LaPierre says. "No one else has been in the house."

"I can't imagine anyone would break into someone's house just to take a doll and put it in front of the window," I say. "Seems like a lot of work just to try and scare someone."

"Can we see the doll?" Beth asks.

"Of course," Mrs. LaPierre says. She stands up and motions for us to come with her. We all get up and follow her through the living room and into a small bedroom off of the main hallway.

As soon as I step inside, I gasp. Literally hundreds of doll heads stare off in every direction. The room is full of dolls. They're up on shelves. They're lined up along the walls. Some sit. Some stand.

"Wow," I say.

"It's a bit of an obsession," Mrs. LaPierre admits. She stands there for a moment and looks around at all of the dolls as if admiring them.

"Maybe the doll just wanted some privacy," Hai whispers to me.

Beth squeezes between Hai and me and then maneuvers around the small twin bed in the middle of the room. She places her hand on the shoulder of a dark-haired doll that sits underneath the shelf.

I can't help but think about how those same hands rested on my own shoulders at last night's dance.

"It's this one, right?" Beth says. I'm amazed for a moment before I remember that the doll did come from Days Gone Buy. Beth must've seen it before it was sold.

"Yes," Mrs. LaPierre says. "That was where I put it right after I brought it home from your parents' store. I've been gone for a week, but I came back early this morning and found it standing upstairs, staring out the window."

Beth's face tightens.

It feels like the room has changed, like it's gotten slightly cooler somehow. That's what it does when something paranormal is about to happen.

I don't know how we'd explain to Mrs. LaPierre that there's probably a ghost haunting the newest doll in her collection.

"I don't like this," Hai whispers. "I swear that all of these dolls could come alive any second."

"If you don't mind," Beth says feebly, "I'd like to take this back to the store for a while."

"Yes, that would be fine," Mrs. LaPierre says. "I've had an uneasy feeling ever since I found it by the window. I was going to return the doll, but do you think you can fix it?"

Beth pauses for a second, as if she's at a loss for words.

"I can sometimes make stuff stop . . . misbehaving," Beth says. "It's actually hard to explain."

It's dead silent in the bedroom of dolls, but I'd bet Mrs. LaPierre knows exactly what Beth means. She just doesn't want to say it.

Heck, even I don't want to say it.

There's a ghost stuck inside the old doll, and Beth needs to talk to it.

Here's the thing about Days Gone Buy: They've already sold a few items from Red's haunted antique pile in the basement. I don't know how many other pieces are scattered around Two Mile Creek, but we've been the ones to solve the mysteries behind the objects. The staring doll is number four.

We've done our best to hold back words like "haunted" and "ghost" when dealing with customers who've purchased the items. The reason? Word spreads fast in a small town.

If people in Two Mile Creek catch on that the Markles are selling haunted stuff to their customers, no one will shop there anymore. The store could lose business and close, and then Beth and her family could move to some other town to start over.

I can't let that happen, especially not now.

But how can we explain to someone why their doll is walking through the house only to park itself in front of a window? We can't. That's why I'm thinking we're in trouble.

As we head down Mrs. LaPierre's front walk with the doll, I wonder if she's already on the phone, gossiping.

"I'd offer to carry it," Hai says as we walk past my house. "But that dolly creeps me out like you would not believe."

Beth shrugs, holding the doll at the waist and cradling her head. "It's fine," she says. "It's really fragile anyway."

"Well, it's not like I'd drop it," Hai says. "You know, unless it started talking or moving."

"Did you sense anything?" I ask. "Back at the house?"

"Yes," Beth says. "There's a woman trapped inside this doll."

"She's in the doll right now?" Hai says. "Like right this second?"

"Yes," Beth says. "I'm afraid so. I just don't know who it is yet."

The doll's face has those eyes that close when it's lying down and open when it's sitting or standing up.

With each footstep Beth takes, the eyes flutter. I have to look away and focus somewhere else. Dolls, in general, are a bit terrifying, but knowing a ghost is stuck inside this one makes it even worse.

"Should we find Liz?" I say. "Maybe she can find out who used to own the doll."

The Markle twins found an old journal that once belonged to Red in the basement, near his haunted collection. He cataloged every item in the place and who owned it before he got his hands on it. The journal has been helpful for some of our investigations.

"Let's go to the library and have Liz meet us there," Beth says. "I don't want to bring this back to the store. My parents will wonder why we keep coming back with antiques we've already sold."

"Maybe we should tell them," I say. "Let them know the stuff in the basement is haunted, and they shouldn't sell it. Look at all the trouble it's causing."

"I can't," Beth says, looking off. "I'm not supposed to. I've been told that no one else should know."

"Who told you that?" I asked. Now I'm really confused.

"I don't really know," Beth says, shaking her head. "But I just feel like I shouldn't tell. Besides, I don't want my parents to know about my . . . gift."

"If I got that as a gift, I'd ask for the gift receipt," Hai says.

When I wince, he smirks.

"I'll call Liz," Hai says. He pulls out his cell phone and finds her number. As he's talking to her on the phone, I turn to Beth.

"Any idea why she's trapped inside the doll?" I ask. I still feel like she should say something to her parents, but I don't push it.

I keep my eyes on Beth and not the haunted toy in her arms. The wind picks up just then, making the doll's long, shiny red dress flap.

"No," Beth says. "But whoever is here with us is hurt, clinging to our world for as long as she can."

"We just don't know why," I say quietly.

"Not yet," Beth says. She offers up a small smile.

I think about the old wagon we investigated previously. The ghost of Peter Whittle stuck around to make amends with his still-living younger brother, Arnold. Was the woman in the doll doing the same thing? Was that how some ghosts ended up trapped here? To seek forgiveness?

"Liz will meet us there," Hai says and pockets his phone. "She didn't sound too excited about it, though."

She never does, I think to myself.

It's about twenty minutes later, and Liz still hasn't shown up yet. We're all sitting over near the giant stained glass windows in our town library, waiting. We're unsure where to even start. In the past, we've asked for the librarian, Mrs. Gulliver's, help. But she's probably in the back room, sorting out the book returns, and we don't want to bug her.

The library is mostly quiet, except for the odd creaks and faint music coming from the record player at the front of the library. I look over at the doll, sitting like a smaller person in the chair across the table from me. Chills tickle my skin just looking at the porcelain-faced girl, but Beth seems okay sitting next to it.

"Is Claudette around?" Hai asks. He's gazing up at the ceiling as if the library's ghost might appear above us any second.

"Oh, she's here," Beth whispers. "I don't think she's going anywhere."

Claudette is a ghost we helped that was attached to an old phonograph. She didn't want to leave until she heard her favorite song. And even after she did hear it, she still didn't go anywhere. Since Claudette and Mrs. Gulliver were friends growing up, the librarian bought the old record player, so they could hang out together in the library.

Just then, the front door squeaks open, and a wide blast of light is cast through the mostly empty library. Heavy footsteps approach, and it doesn't take a brainiac to figure out Liz has finally arrived.

"Wow," Liz says, hitching a thumb behind her. "That ghost is *still* listening to that old song?"

As she says that, what feels like an arctic wind blows through the library. A framed poster hanging on the wall rattles against the plaster. It features a girl from the 1970s with a finger over her mouth, reminding everyone to keep quiet.

"You're upsetting Claudette," Beth whispers.

"And you, Beth, are upsetting me by being so creepy," Liz replies.

"Okay, okay," I say. "Let's be nice, all right? What did you find in the journal?"

Liz holds the beat-up, leather bound book up. "That doll used to belong to Marla Darling."

"Darling?" Hai says. "What kind of name is that?"

A cold, heavy presence settles over me, and I'm sure everyone else feels it, too. All of us watch in horror as the doll's head turns slightly to stare at my best friend with those shiny, empty eyes.

Hai screams, beating me to it, actually.

"What is going on over here?" says Mrs. Gulliver as she hurries over. She's adjusting the eyeglasses she has hanging from a thin chain around her neck. She's looking but not seeing.

Hai is pointing at the doll. Liz has hidden under the table. I'm speechless, and my heart pounds. The only one who doesn't seem frazzled by all of this is Beth.

"We're sorry, Mrs. Gulliver," Beth says, her

face calm despite the commotion. "We just wanted to —"

"Is that . . ." Mrs. Gulliver says, interrupting Beth.

The librarian stalks over to where the doll sits, the head still cocked in Hai's direction. She reaches toward the doll and very gently touches the toy's curly hair. I'd call out to warn her of an attack if I could find my voice.

". . . a *Darling* doll?" Mrs. Gulliver says.

"If you say so," Hai says, breathing hard.

Liz's head pops up from underneath the table. "Darling was the last name of the lady who owned that doll."

Mrs. Gulliver stands up and holds her hands beneath her chin, steeple-like. After a moment, she parts the doll's hair and waves us over.

I almost don't want to get up and see, but if Hai and Liz are going, I should too.

"This is a Darling Doll," Mrs. Gulliver says. She points to a spot on the porcelain skull and sure enough, written in cursive letters are the words *DARLING DOLL*.

"I don't get it," I say. "So the doll and the owner have the same name?"

"This doll was made right here in Two Mile Creek," Mrs. Gulliver explains. "Here, let me show you."

Mrs. Gulliver takes us through the shelves and stacks of books to a small section in the reference section.

"Back when Two Mile Creek was a thriving town, there were a lot more businesses around," Mrs. Gulliver explains. "One of them was a small company where handmade dolls were lovingly created. It was named after the owner of the doll shop."

"Did her name happen to be Marla?" Liz asks. "Because that's who owned the scary little monster sitting at the table."

By way of a response, Mrs. Gulliver opens a book full of historical black and white photos of our town. She flips through a number of pages before turning it toward us.

"The Darling Doll Company," I say, reading the tiny caption beneath the picture.

The photo shows an old house with a storefront built onto it. Standing in front of the place is a thin, dark-haired woman. She's holding a doll in front of her that has long blond hair and a green dress.

The Darling Doll Company
Marla Darling, proprietor

"Marla Darling, proprietor," Beth reads, moving closer to me to get a better view. I don't mind at all.

"So Marla *is* the owner," Liz says. "Is her shop still in business?"

"Oh, no," Mrs. Gulliver says. "Like a lot of the businesses here in town, Darling Dolls had to close its doors. I suppose that when jobs dried up in Two Mile Creek, people couldn't afford expensive toys like fancy dolls. It was unfortunate, really. Marla really did some beautiful work."

"Hey, look at the small girl standing off to the side," I say.

"It's as if she's trying to stay out of the picture," says Beth.

"Weird," I say. "Or, like, sad, I guess."

"Did you ever have one of those dolls, Mrs. G.?" Hai asks.

"I'm afraid not," Mrs. Gulliver says. "Nothing like that for me. Those dolls were far too expensive for my family. A few of the girls from school did, but not many. People used to come to Two Mile Creek and commission Marla to make them. That's how well-known those unique dolls were."

"Commission?" I ask. I guess I'm not sure what that means.

"Sure," Mrs. Gulliver says. "They'd hire Marla to make one special for them. Some had a doll made in their daughter's likeness. That way she'd have a dolly version of herself."

"Okay," Liz says. "That's officially horrifying."

Mrs. Gulliver shrugs. "It was quite remarkable back in the day. Now factories can easily make a plastic version of anything, but the Darling Doll Company handcrafted those beautiful porcelain faces. There were never two alike. Just like real people, I suppose."

So true, I think. The Markle twins are supposed to be alike, but they're as different as sandpaper and sunshine.

"Thanks for showing this to us," Beth says. Her voice is quiet, like she's afraid she'll wake someone up. "But I'm not sure how this helps us with our doll out there."

Mrs. Gulliver cranes her neck around the shelf.

"Oh," she says quickly. "Oh, my. I'm afraid your doll is gone, dear."

Almost immediately, a cold sensation brushes past my cheek. I don't know if it's Claudette's ghost flying through the library unseen or if it's just the fear rising through my body. Everyone around me seems afraid to even breathe.

I take a couple of cautious steps forward and peer around the shelves, too. Sure enough, the seat where we left the Darling Doll is empty. The chair is moved out a bit, as if a real person had edged it back to stand up.

"Casey?" Beth asks. "Is it true?"

"Yeah," I whisper, feeling my voice shudder. "She's gone."

Though I really don't think anyone stole the doll, I almost wish that's the case. Maybe it's because Beth is watching me, but I've become foolishly brave somehow, so I venture out into the otherwise empty library.

"You're crazy, Willis!" Hai whispers, hiding behind Beth and Liz.

A moment later, Beth slips out, too, following closely behind me. Not to be outdone by her timid twin sister, Liz follows.

"Is there something you're not telling me about this particular doll?" Mrs. Gulliver asks. I realize that, in her excitement over seeing the doll, we never mentioned the antique doll was haunted.

"There's a spirit clinging to it," Beth says. "Like Claudette's record player."

"It seems the four of you are making a habit of this sort of business," Mrs. Gulliver says, following us from the shelves.

"Not by choice," Liz says. "My sister is really friendly with ghosts."

"A *sensitive* you mean," Mrs. Gulliver says.

"No," Liz says. "I think she's a freakshow."

I want to tell Liz not be so mean to Beth, but I'm nearly as timid about speaking to her as I am to Beth.

"You think someone stole the doll?" Hai asks, following us. "Maybe? Guys?"

I don't answer him, trying to keep quiet as I peer around the shelf of large print books and down the main aisle. I hear a small tapping sound. "Does anyone else hear little footsteps?" I ask.

"Like doll footsteps?" Hai asks. He shakes his head in terrified disbelief.

"We won't hurt you," Beth says into the air. "I promise."

I really hope the doll doesn't answer back.

All of us pause for a moment and listen. It's dead silent for a moment before the footsteps start up again.

"The periodicals," Mrs. Gulliver says. "This way."

We follow the librarian through the rows of books. I just know my skin will leap off of my skeleton if I see doll's face peering through the shelves at me or if a tiny porcelain hand grabs my ankle.

We all walk really close together, and since I'm right next to Beth, our shoulders touch.

"There," Mrs. Gulliver whispers and comes to a full stop. We're right behind her, so we bump into the older lady, almost knocking her over. I'm afraid to see what she sees, but I look anyway.

Standing at the window, overlooking the small, empty Two Mile Creek Library parking lot, is the doll. It stares out the window as if hypnotized. Immediately, I see Beth's hand go to her forehead, and she squeezes her eyes tight behind her glasses.

"Are you okay?" I ask.

"She's in pain," Beth whispers. "I can't understand what she's saying, but something is wrong."

"Everything is wrong," Liz says. "There's a ghost living inside a scary doll's body!"

Without another word, Beth walks over to the window. When she gets there, she rests her hand against the doll's back.

"It's okay," Beth says. "We'll help you."

The doll continues to stare.

I walk to the window and peer out into the parking lot. I check out every inch of the cracked pavement that I can see from the window, but nothing jumps out. *What is this doll looking for?*

Adjusting my view, I realize I can make out the eastern end of town through the trees that line the street across from the library. There's a building out there.

"What's she looking at, Casey?" Hai asks, keeping as far away from the doll as possible.

I'm squinting through the sun coming in through the dusty window, trying to figure out what I'm seeing. The only places I can think of over there are Mitchell & Sons Hardware store, the Creamy King ice cream place and . . .

"Dolly's Diner," I whisper.

"Seriously?" Liz says. "Are you kidding?"

Beth is zoning out as if she's hearing voices we can't. "Yes," Beth says. "That's it."

Mrs. Gulliver exhales long and loud. It's like someone vacuumed the wind out of her lungs.

"I know the history behind Dolly's," the librarian says, joining us at the window.

"Okay," I say. "What's the deal with that place?"

"Before Dolly's was a restaurant," Mrs. Gulliver says, "it was the Darling Doll Company."

"They started a restaurant business instead?" I ask. "Seems like an awfully big change to go from doll-making to flipping burgers."

Mrs. Gulliver laughs and then pats me on the back.

"Not quite, Casey," she says. "After Marla passed away, Bernie Sullivan bought the place and turned it into a diner. This was a few decades back now. Because Darling Dolls was regarded as a landmark to our town, he paid it homage by naming it Dolly's."

"Dolly's Diner," Liz says. "Makes sense to me, I guess."

"I don't think you understand how incredibly well-known these dolls were," Mrs. Gulliver says. "It was hard to see Marla's company go out of business. People around here felt like a piece of their history was gone. In an instant, an institution in our little town just disappeared."

I'd been to Dolly's plenty of times, but I never thought to find out why it was named that. I guess I always assumed a previous owner had been named Dolly. I think it's obvious what we need to do next.

"I guess we're taking the dolly over to Dolly's Diner," I say. "If that's where the doll wants to be."

◆

Dolly's Diner doesn't look much like the picture back at the library. The small house where Marla Darling ran her small company is set behind the actual diner itself. I never even noticed the house back there. Instead of leveling the place, Mr. Sullivan just added the dining area to the front.

"The diner's closed," Hai says, pointing at the sign hanging in the window. "They don't open until 11 for lunch."

"It's, like, ten minutes until eleven," Liz says, looking at her sports watch. "Should we wait? This whole plan seems dumb to me."

As no one has a better plan, we wait. Hai messes with an app on his phone. Beth seems lost in her own head, making me wonder if the ghost is trying to tell her something.

So as we're standing here, holding an expensive antique doll, a fancy black car drives by. The window goes down, and someone shouts at us.

"Nice doll, Willis!"

I don't see who it is, but I have a good idea. It's probably Muffleman, still upset about the Spring Fever Dance last night.

"Hey!" Hai yells after the car as it turns the corner at the end of the block. "This doll would give you nightmares, man!"

I hear a muffled jingling noise and turn to see Bernie Sullivan behind the glass front door of the diner. He's twisting the keys to unlock the door with one hand and flipping the CLOSED sign to OPEN with the other. It seems our waiting period is over.

"Who's hungry?" Liz asks, nodding toward the restaurant.

"If that doll says, *I am,*" Hai says, "then I'm outta here."

Since we're the first ones in the door of Dolly's Diner, we get our pick of the tables. I sit on the inside, next to Hai, but across from Beth who bookends the doll's spot along with Liz. The bottom half of the doll's face is blocked by the table. Even so, it seems like her eyes are staring at me.

"Thanks for coming in, gang," Mr. Sullivan says, dropping off some menus and silverware at our table.

Before we can respond, he points at the doll. "Is that what I think it is?" he asks.

"Yeah," Liz says, acting like it's no big deal. "It's one of those Darling Dolls they used to make here. We figured we'd take her out on the town, let her see her birthplace."

"Wow, she's in good shape," Mr. Sullivan says, whistling. "My mom had three of those back in the day. They're worth a fortune."

"So," I say, "the Darling Dolls Company used to be here, right?"

"That's right," Mr. Sullivan says. "Miss Marla used to live in the house and had a small workshop in the basement where she made each and every doll on her own. Since she could only make so many of them, they were a bit expensive."

"Strange that she never had a factory built," Hai says. "Maybe business would've been better."

Mr. Sullivan shrugs. "Maybe," he says. "But that's what made them special. She put a lot of heart and soul into her dolls. I believe she did it for the art and not for the money."

"Yes, I think you're right," Beth says. It seems like she's trying to hold a grimace in, but she manages to give Mr. Sullivan a weak smile.

"My cook isn't here yet, so holler when you're ready to order," Mr. Sullivan says. He slips back behind the counter, where stools are lined up just like diners from the old days. I watch as he wipes the counter with a rag and adjusts a napkin dispenser that looks over-stuffed.

"So this is a waste of time," Liz says, slouching back in her seat.

"Yeah," Hai says. "Why'd she want to come here? To meet up with other dolls?"

"Downstairs," Beth whispers as she leans in toward the middle of the table. "We need to take her downstairs."

I glance over at Mr. Sullivan who is unfolding a newspaper.

"Really?" I ask. "How can we do that? Mr. Sullivan lives here, now."

Beth nods as if she understands, but we need to do it anyway.

We all sit for a moment in silence, and I turn to check the place out. I really have no idea where the house connects to the diner.

All I see through the kitchen is the order window where slips of paper are usually hung to show the cooks what food the customers have ordered. There's a large metal stove with a vent hood above it. A bunch of metal pots and utensils rest on a metal counter.

Toward the back, I spot a wooden door, just inside the kitchen. A black sticker with gold letters on the door says *PRIVATE* and another below it reads *WATCH YOUR STEP*.

"It might be in there," I say, tilting my head. "See that door?"

"Well," Liz says. "Do we ask him if we can check it out? I'm not sure he's going to let the bunch of us down there."

"What if he says no?" I ask. "Then we're really stuck."

"You think we should sneak down there, Casey?" Hai asks. "Like secret-agent style?"

"Well," I say. "If going into the basement of an old diner is what second-rate secret agents do, then yeah, maybe."

The front door opens and an older couple walks in. They wave to Mr. Sullivan, and he goes over to greet them. They seem to know him pretty well and begin chatting him up.

"His back is to us," Liz says. "If we're going to go, we better go now."

My heart beats like a heavy metal drum solo. I slip out of the booth and very carefully make my way to the opening at the dining counter. Mr. Sullivan is laughing with the old guy, and the older lady sitting with him shakes her head.

I duck into the kitchen and head toward the door. I turn to see that Beth has the doll and everyone else is close behind. We all crouch down so that we can't be seen through the order window and pass between a prep table and a large industrial refrigerator.

At the door, I reach for the knob, hoping and praying it isn't locked. I give the door knob a quick twist, and it turns in my hand. I open it up and peer inside. An old set of wooden steps leads into the darkness.

"We're in business," I say holding the door open. One by one, we all head inside, and then making sure the coast is clear, I follow, closing the door behind me.

Hai's uses his cell phone as a flashlight as we dig around the basement, dimly illuminated by light coming in through dirty windows.

I was expecting to see some old doll heads, sewing machines, and fabric everywhere, but instead, we've discovered the diner's storage room. Boxes of Styrofoam cups, placemats, soft drink syrup boxes, and industrial-sized plastic jugs of ketchup and mustard cram the shelves.

Any trace of Marla Darling's doll workshop is long gone.

"Okay," Liz says. "So do you think the doll just wanted to see where they keep the ketchup? What're we doing here, guys?""

"We probably don't have much time," I say, watching Beth. "Is this where we need to be?"

"Yes, they're here," she says in a haunted whisper that sounds almost nothing like her.

"Oh, man," Hai says. "Who's here? Her creepy doll army? We're going to totally get attacked by a bunch of broken-faced dolls, aren't we?"

"What does she mean?" I ask concentrating on Beth. "Who's here?"

"We have to find them," Beth says. "She hid them, and we have to find them."

I walk around, trying to figure out what the ghost in the doll could possibly mean. Besides the restaurant supplies, all we've found are a few broken chairs and a furnace that looks older than my grandpa.

"Keep looking," I say. "Maybe we'll know it when we see it."

Beth sets the doll on the floor next to a shelf with sugar dispensers on it. The doll's pleasant but expressionless face stares off into nowhere.

I peek into some of the boxes, hoping to find some remnants of the past that existed here before Dolly's Diner was built. One carton contains a bunch of paper napkins. Another is full of salt and pepper packets.

"I'm not finding anything," Hai says. Above us, heavy footsteps make the floor creak. Mr. Sullivan is back in the kitchen and probably wondering where we've gone.

"What is she saying, Beth?" I ask. I'm feeling panicky, thinking maybe this was a dumb idea.

Beth shakes her head. As she does, the basement cools down considerably as if a huge draft were let in. The shelves begin to shake and rumble. A box of soft drink lids falls to the floor. I put it back on the shelf while Liz and Hai start backing toward the wooden steps.

"I can't make out a whole lot," Beth says. "Only that they're here."

Liz stares up toward the top of the stairs and then back at her twin sister. "It would be nice," Liz says, "if these ghosts, for once, would just point us in the right direction!"

And just like that, the doll's right arm rises and points toward a dark corner in the room. My breath gets stuck down in my throat, and Hai stumbles and falls backward against the steps, landing on his rear end.

"Okay," Liz whispers. "I'm keeping my mouth shut forever now."

I walk toward the dark corner and find even more boxes stacked on shelves. I really hope there isn't another doll, ghost, or any other horrible creature waiting to grab at me.

Beth, following behind me, trips and falls to the ground.

"Are you okay?" I ask. I help her up by grabbing her hand.

"Yeah," Beth says, glancing quickly behind her. "I just . . . fell."

Ever since I've met her, I noticed that Beth is clumsy at times, but there's something in her face that seems different. I'm about to ask what she's seeing or hearing when the basement door opens. The rumbling shelves instantly stop shaking.

"Guys," Liz whispers. "We're busted!"

8

"Hello?" Mr. Sullivan's voice calls from the diner's kitchen.

I move toward the dark corner, ignoring Mr. Sullivan and the panicky feeling in my chest. Beth is right with me, and we peer into the gap between the shelf and the corner.

"I can't see what's back there," I say. "Hai, bring your phone over here."

Hai tosses the phone over, and I catch it. I shine it into the corner to reveal a dusty floor.

I hear Liz slink over toward us, her shoes scraping the gritty basement tiles.

"There has to be something," I say, looking up and down the wall. At the floor, I notice two pieces of wood joined together at the corner. One of them isn't nailed very securely. I reach down and slip my fingers behind the wood and pull. The piece comes away easily.

"That's it," Beth whispers.

Behind us, the steps creak with Mr. Sullivan's approaching steps.

Getting down on my knees, I clear the wood away to find a small bundle of papers. I pull them out to reveal a bunch of yellowed envelopes.

Mr. Sullivan is at the bottom of the steps now. "Are you kids down here?" he says.

Not knowing what else to do, I stand up and stuff the letters into the front pocket of my hooded sweatshirt.

"What are you doing down here?" he asks, staring at everyone like we've eaten the last bite of his favorite sandwich.

I need to think quickly. I spot a bunch of toilet paper on another shelf and the words just tumble out. "Toilet," I say. "We were looking for the bathroom."

There's an uncomfortable moment of silence before Mr. Sullivan responds. I can't tell if he believes all four of us would need to go to the bathroom at the same time or if he's considering calling the police.

"It's upstairs near the front," he says. He glances around as if to see if his stock is out of place or missing.

"Oh, okay," I say. "Sorry. We should go, guys."

Beth picks up the doll as Mr. Sullivan follows us up the stairs and out through the kitchen to our table.

"So, where did you say that bathroom was?" I ask.

"I said it's upstairs," Mr. Sullivan says, pointing.

Liz grabs Beth's arm and they hurry off, leaving Hai and I with Mr. Sullivan, who stares at us skeptically. I manage a weak smile.

"Have you two decided on lunch?" he asks.

Hai snaps into action. "Oh, shoot," he says, holding up his phone. "My mom just texted me. Could we get some cookies to go?"

Mr. Sullivan's eyes narrow.

Hai smiles his most innocent smile.

"Cookies, huh?" he says. "Sure. We have chocolate chip."

"Perfect," I say. "We'll take four."

A minute later, we're out the front door with our sack of cookies, each of us feeling like we escaped a close call.

When we're a good two blocks from Dolly's Diner and out of sight, I pull the bundle of papers out of my sweatshirt pocket.

"Looks like letters," Hai says. "Old letters."

I turn over the stack of yellowed envelopes in my hand. They're tied together with a thin piece of twine. The letter on top hasn't been opened, is addressed to DOROTHY DARLING, and is stamped RETURN TO SENDER.

Since we're near Liberty Park, our town's only public park and a popular picnic spot, I spy an empty picnic table and lead our group over before digging deeper into the bundled letters.

I drop the stack onto the tabletop's peeling wood and sit down. Beth gently sets the doll at the end of the table. Hai and Liz gather round, still chomping at their cookies. A couple of kids are flying back and forth on the old swing set while a toddler climbs up onto the end of a slide.

I untie the twine and spread the letters out. I count nine of them in total. All of them are addressed to Dorothy Darling. Some of the most recent ones were sent to an address in Colorado. The return address is also the same on each letter: M. DARLING from the same street address as Dolly's Diner.

"So we did all of that," Liz says. "For some cookies and a bunch of old letters someone else didn't want?"

"Well, yeah," I say with a shrug. "But the doll wanted us to find them for some reason."

"Don't remind me," Liz says. She visibly shivers, and I know she's recalling the doll pointing to the corner.

"None of them are opened," Hai says through a mouthful of cookie. "What's up with that?"

"We need to find out who Dorothy Darling is," I say.

"Marla's mom?" offers Liz. "Marla's sister?"

Out of the corner of my eye, I see Beth touching the doll's porcelain hand. Beth's eyes are squeezed shut as if she's concentrating.

"We need to read these," Beth says.

"It's kind of weird reading someone else's mail, isn't it?" Hai says. "Isn't that like private property or —"

"Marla wants us to read them," Beth says.

"So the woman who made these dolls," Liz says. "Is stuck inside this one?"

"Yes," Beth says.

I'm not sure why I didn't consider that Marla Darling could be the ghost living inside the doll. The notion gives me goose bumps.

Though it feels slightly wrong to be opening someone else's mail, I carefully tear open the envelope of the letter that was on top. I lay it out on the table, and we all take a moment to read it.

Dorothy,

I'm writing to you in hopes that you'll be able to forgive me. I've never wanted to drive you away and become a stranger to you. Having all of this time apart has made me realize how awful life must have been with me. I understand why you wanted to leave. No mother ever wants to become estranged from her daughter, but I fear that's exactly what has happened. I haven't heard from you in months, Dottie. Please come home so that we can talk.

I love you,

Mother

"So Marla is Dorothy's mom," I say, rereading parts of the letter.

We open other letters. Liz holds up one that includes a photograph.

"This one talks about the last doll she ever made," Liz says, her eyes watery. Could it be that Liz actually has a heart after all?

Liz holds up the photo to show us. In it, an older Marla Darling holds a doll. The same doll lying on the picnic table two feet from me.

"The doll is Dorothy," says Liz. "The letter says that her last doll was of her own daughter."

"We need to reach her," Beth whispers, still holding the doll's hand. "That's what Marla wants. That's what she's wanted all along."

I open another envelope and read another plea from Marla for her daughter to forgive her and come back home. She mentions that the drive to keep the company running is gone without her. In another, Marla talks about the impending doom of the Darling Doll Company.

I can't do this without you, the letter says. *All that matters to me is you.*

"I wonder what happened," I whisper to Beth.

Beth slowly shakes her head and presses her lips together. I guess Marla isn't telling her.

Hai holds up his phone. "I'm glad Darling isn't a really common name," Hai says. "If the lady I found on the internet is the same Dorothy from the letters, her name is now Dorothy Everett. Looks like she got married and has two kids in Colorado."

"You want to call?" I ask.

Hai shakes his head.

Beth reaches out for the phone. "I'll do it," she says.

Hai dials up the number and hands the phone to Beth. We hold our breath, wondering if she's going to reach the right person.

"Put it on speakerphone, Beth," Liz says.

Beth squints at the phone.

Hai reaches over and pushes a button, and then we hear the line ringing. After two more rings, someone picks up.

"Hello?" It's a woman's voice.

"Hi," Beth says. "Is this Dorothy?"

"Yes, it is," the woman says. "Who's calling, please?"

"Hi Dorothy," Beth says. "My name is Beth Markle. I live in Two Mile Creek. I hope I'm not bothering you, but did your name used to be Dorothy Darling?"

There's a pause on the line.

"It was," Dorothy says. "Yes."

"My parents run an antique store in town," says Beth. "We've recently found the doll your mom made to look like you and —"

"Where did you get this number?" Dorothy asks.

"I don't mean to make you angry," Beth says. "I just think your mom wants to —"

And just like that the phone beeps. The call is disconnected.

Beth lowers the phone and looks at it. Hai reaches for it, but Beth shakes her head. "I'm going to call her back," she says.

"Beth," says Liz. "Let it go. I don't think she wants to talk about it."

"She needs to hear what I have to say," says Beth. She holds the phone to her ear.

I want to stop her, too. I'm afraid Dorothy is only going to get angrier if we keep pestering her. After a few seconds, Beth speaks.

"Hello, Mrs. Everett," Beth says, still holding the doll's hand. "It's Beth Markle again. I'm sorry to leave this on your voice mail, but I need to tell you this. We've made contact with your mother, Marla."

Hai, Liz, and I all stare at Beth.

"She told me that she's sorry for shutting you out," Beth continues. "You mom never meant to make you feel like second-best and only wants your forgiveness."

Where is Beth getting this info? How does she know all these things?

"I can't pretend to know what you've gone through," Beth continues. "But your Mom misses you and only wants to be at rest, knowing that you hear her apology. She says her world has been empty without you and that she would change the past if she could."

Beth's eyes are closed, and she's pinching the small hand even tighter.

"I'm sorry I drove you away, Dottie honey," Beth says in a voice that doesn't like Beth.

We sit there, stunned.

"A broken doll is nothing compared to my broken heart," Beth says. "I love you." She holds the phone away from her face and ends the call. "Okay," Beth says in her normal voice as she hands the phone back. "We did everything we could."

"What," Liz says slowly. "The. Heck."

I have so many questions that I don't know where to begin. But I can tell Beth's exhausted. The unexplainable just happened when she held the Darling Doll's hand.

"Um, did we just hear Marla's voice?" asks Hai. "Like, through you?"

"Marla is still here," Beth says, ignoring the question. "So maybe she won't be able to let go. Or doesn't want to."

"Do we bring the doll back to Mrs. LaPierre?" I ask. "Maybe it won't stare off toward Dolly's Diner now that we have the letters. Won't that be good enough?"

"Let's give it some time," Beth says. "We can take the doll back to the store and see what happens. If the doll stays put, we'll bring it back to her."

"We need to hide that doll somewhere," Liz says. "If Mom and Dad see us with that thing, they're going to flip."

I collect the letters and stick them back in the envelopes. I bundle them all together and tie them up before handing them to Liz. Beth scoops up the doll in her arms. We all stand there for a moment watching the haunted antique.

"I'm sorry we couldn't do more," Beth says, looking the doll in the eyes. "We tried."

The doll stares silently up into the clouds.

It's Sunday afternoon, and I'm doing my math homework. I'm hoping for any excuse not to finish it since I'm practically falling asleep looking through the list of problems. I don't even hear the phone ring, but my mom comes into my room.

"Hey, Casey," Mom says. "You've got a call."

She hands me the cordless phone.

"Hello?" I say.

"Casey?" the sweet, angelic voice on the other end says. "It's Beth. Can you and Hai come to the store? Mrs. LaPierre called. We're going to sneak the doll out and bring it to her."

"Won't your parents see?" I ask.

"They're out making a delivery," Beth says. "If we hurry, we can get it out of here."

"I'm on my way," I say. "I'll call Hai and have him meet us."

"Perfect," she says. "See you soon."

I smile. I know it's sappy to be all happy just talking to Beth. But I like that she called and needs my help.

Hai and I knock on the front door of Days Gone Buy. It's a few minutes past four o' clock, which is closing time.

A moment later, Liz comes over and unlocks the door. "Get in here," she says, pulling us inside.

"What are we doing?" I ask, glancing around the store. "Shouldn't we go?"

"Beth is just cleaning the doll's dress," Liz says. "We had to tuck it under the stairs in the basement. It got really dusty."

I really hope she hurries. If Mom and Dad Markle get back before we can leave for Mrs. LaPierre's house, we're in for it.

"So why exactly did you need us?" Hai asks. "I mean, it's not like the doll is too heavy to lift alone."

"How should I know?" Liz says. "Beth says we should all be here for it. Like we're a team or whatever."

I smile. Hai shrugs.

Beth scurries up, holding the doll. "Thanks for coming, guys," she says. "We should go."

Just as we step out of the store, a big red SUV pulls up along the curb.

"Uh-oh," Liz whispers.

Beth and Liz's parents are in the car.

Mrs. Markle is out of the car and in front of us before the engine even stops. Mr. Markle isn't far behind.

"What are you girls doing with that doll?" Mrs. Markle asks.

"Do you have any idea how expensive that is?" Mr. Markle says.

"It's a long story, Dad," Beth says. "And I can't explain it right now, but —"

"Why not?" Mrs. Markle asks. She places her hands on her hips. She's expecting an answer.

We're all silent, not sure what to say to explain ourselves.

"We're bringing it back to Mrs. LaPierre," Beth says.

"We sold that doll to her last week, Beth," Mrs. Markle says. "And I think I deserve to know why my daughters have it back at our store."

Beth looks at Liz and then me. No one seems prepared to respond, so I speak up. I just hope I don't regret it.

"There's a ghost living inside this doll," I say. Once the words are out of my mouth, I realize how ridiculous that sounds.

"Excuse me?" Mr. Markle says. "You'll have to repeat that."

We're all quiet and looking at each other, expecting someone to speak up. I'm really wishing I hadn't said anything because the silence is crazy awkward. The Markle twins look at each other as if they're both struggling with what to say. I'm about to open my dumb mouth again when, surprisingly, Liz beats me to it.

"It's true, Dad," Liz says. "We've been selling haunted stuff to people since we've opened the store. This is the fourth item we've found that has a spirit attached to it."

"Wait, wait," Mrs. Markle says. She's shaking her head and pinching the top of her nose with her fingertips. "If any of this were even true, how would you even know this?"

The silence that follows her question stretches out.

"Because I can talk to them," Beth says softly. She's gazing down at the sidewalk like she's ashamed. "I can sense when they're near and when they need our help."

"Oh, Bethany," Mrs. Markle says. "That's insane. There aren't such things as ghosts."

"There is," Hai says. "And I have proof."

Before I can stop him, Hai has his phone out. He presses the screen a few times and holds it out for the Markles to watch.

"What is . . . " Mr. Markle begins. "Hey, that's our store."

It doesn't take me long to realize what he's showing them. It's the video from when we helped the ghostly goalie out. Hai filmed us trying to talk to the ghost of Gordon Williams, and in the video you can clearly see a shadowy figure walking behind Beth as we tried to learn his name.

"What is that?" Mrs. Markle says with a gasp. "Oh, my lord."

"That can't be real," Mr. Markle says, but his face is pale, and his mouth hangs open.

"It's real," Liz says. "Beth has been able to do this ever since we moved here."

Beth's parents look at her as if seeing her for the first time. She meets their eyes and then sighs before nodding at the Darling Doll in her arm.

"I don't know how it happened," Beth says, "or why it has to be me. But we tried to help the soul stuck inside this doll."

"Why didn't you tell us?" Mrs. Markle says.

"I don't know," Beth says. "I was afraid of what you would think."

"The truth is," I say, feeling everyone's eyes on me. "We didn't know what would happen to the store if people in town heard you were selling haunted antiques. We were afraid word would get around, and people would stop shopping here."

Mr. and Mrs. Markle look at me.

"I don't want the store to close down," I say. "I'd like you guys to stick around for a while."

Mr. Markle crosses his arms. Beth's mom puts her hand on my shoulder. I know they have a million questions. Who wouldn't?

A woman with dark brown hair approaches the store.

"I'm sorry," Mr. Markle calls. "We're closed for the day."

The woman appears tired and worn out. Her eyes are puffy and red as if she'd been crying. "I'm sorry," she says. "But is Beth Markle here?"

"Dorothy?" Beth asks. She slips past us and over to the woman. She's still holding the Darling Doll.

"I'm sorry for hanging up on you yesterday," Dorothy said. "I wasn't ready to think about my mother. My past came rushing back at me, and I got scared. But when I heard your voice mail, I just couldn't ignore it."

"Wait a moment," Mrs. Markle said. "That's my daughter you're talking to. I don't mean to be rude, but who are you?"

"My apologies," Dorothy said. "My name is Dorothy Everett. My mother was Marla Darling, the creator of the Darling Dolls. Your daughter phoned me yesterday, to tell me that my mom was . . ."

"It's okay," Beth says. "They know."

Dorothy takes a deep breath and lets it all out. "This is all too crazy," she says. "But your daughter said things no one could have possibly known. Things that only my mother and I shared."

Beth shifts on her feet as if unsure what to say.

"We found the letters your mom wrote to you," Liz says. "The ones you sent back."

"I didn't want to ever look back," Dorothy says and exhales.

"I'm sorry if our girls and their friends caused you any grief," Mr. Markle says. "We're just now finding out about Beth's . . . talent."

"No, no," Dorothy says. "This was a bandage that needed to be pulled off. I need closure."

Beth lifts the doll up so Dorothy can see it. "This is you," Beth says. "You mom's last doll."

Dorothy picks up the doll, looking it in the eye and staring at its smooth, porcelain face. Her mouth fidgets as if she's fighting back tears again.

"We'll be right back," Mrs. Markle says. "I'll grab some tissues and some coffee."

"Thank you," Dorothy says as a tear streaks from her eye.

Mr. and Mrs. Markle disappear into the store.

"We sold it, but the lady who bought the doll said it was misbehaving," Liz says. "She found it staring off toward your old house, which is a diner now."

"My mother . . . " Dorothy says, "is in here?"

"Yeah," Beth says. "She's right here with us."

"I'm sorry I left," Dorothy says, a tear streaking down her face. "I didn't mean to hurt you. I didn't think you wanted me around anymore."

"She's sorry, too," Beth says. "Sorry she drove you away."

I watch as Dorothy hugs the doll, holding it gently against her. As she does, I notice the doll's eyes close for a moment and then open again.

And while I'm not as sensitive to ghosts as Beth is, I know Marla's ghost is gone.

We're in Dorothy's rental car, and she pulls us up to Mrs. LaPierre's house. It's time to give the doll back to its owner.

Beth and I are in the back, and Mrs. Markle is riding up front in the passenger seat.

"It's this house," I say.

"You've been so polite," Dorothy says. "But I'd like to explain why I left in the first place."

"It's really none of our business," Mrs. Markle says. "You've been through enough without having to — "

"I'd like to," Dorothy says, gently interrupting. "If you'll allow me."

"Yes," Beth says. "We'll listen."

Dorothy explains how her mom made dolls as a hobby, but once people saw her work, it became a full on business. Her mom's obsession with doing all of the work herself eventually drove her dad away, leaving little Dottie with her inattentive mother.

"So she didn't pay much attention to you," I say. "Is that why you were so mad at her?"

"Partly," Dorothy says. "But an accident in her workshop was the final straw."

"What happened?" Beth asks.

Dorothy looks at the doll in her hands, and I can see her thinking back to another time.

"Feeling alone, I went down to her workshop even if Mother was too busy to pay any attention to me. Watching her work, I was brave enough to pick up one of the dolls she was working on —"

Dorothy stops for a moment, shakes her head and lets out a big sigh. This is hard for her.

"I'm sorry," Beth says and puts her hand on Dorothy's shoulder. "You don't have to do this."

"It's fine," Dorothy says. "I need to do this. I had a doll she'd just finished in my arms. While she was working on the clothes, I was playing with it, and it just slipped right through my fingers."

"Oh no," Mrs. Markle whispers.

"The head hit the floor and smashed to pieces," Dorothy says. "I panicked and tried to fix it, but it was no use."

Dorothy pulls a tissue from a holder in between the front seats and wipes her eyes.

"Mother screamed at me like I'd dropped something truly alive," Dorothy says. "From then on, I was banished from her workshop. When I was old enough, I ran away to live with my aunt. If she didn't want me around, I'd leave her alone. Forever."

"I'm sorry that happened to you," Beth says. "She regretted it, but by then, it was too late."

"Thank you," Dorothy says. "I have some regrets, too."

Mrs. Markle wipes her eyes quickly with her hand. "It's so sad to me," she says. "The two of you missed so much of each other's lives. Your graduation, your wedding, the birth of her grandkids, holidays. Even Marla's funeral. It was like neither of you existed to each other anymore."

"It hasn't been easy," Dorothy whispers. She takes a deep breath. "I'd do things differently if I could."

"Are you sure you want to give this doll to Mrs. LaPierre?" I ask. "I mean, the doll is supposed to be you, right?"

Dorothy nods. "It's the fair thing to do," she says.

We get out of the car to offer help, but Mrs. Markle and Dorothy say they're fine bringing the Darling Doll up the walk to Mrs. LaPierre's house. As they do, Beth puts her hand in mine.

"Thank you," Beth says. "For everything, Casey."

"Oh," I say, feeling my face grow warm. "I thought you'd be mad I mentioned the ghosts to your parents. I didn't know what else to do."

"You were right to speak up," Beth says. "I should have talked to them about it a long time ago. But you're always willing to help me, and I'm grateful."

"I'll always help," I say, which is true. "But I'll bet a lot will change from here on out."

"Definitely," Beth says. She squeezes my hand.

I watch as Dorothy hugs Mrs. LaPierre and turns toward the car, with the Darling Doll still in her hand.

"She let her keep it," I say. Knowing now what a huge doll collector my neighbor is, I'm shocked.

"Good," Beth whispers. "Marla wanted her to have it."

The two women get back in the car, and Mrs. LaPierre waves to me. I wave back.

"I've forgotten how nice the people in Two Mile Creek truly are," Dorothy says. "Your neighbor wouldn't take the doll back. She wouldn't accept any money, either."

"We'll give her store credit," Mrs. Markle says. "I know she had her eyes on some of our other items."

"Thank you all again," Dorothy says. "I'll always treasure this day. And now I can bring home a piece of my mother to share with her granddaughters."

I say my goodbyes to everyone, and Beth climbs back in the car. As the silver rental car drives away, Beth turns around in her seat and waves to me from the back window. She smiles at me, and I smile and wave back. I watch the car turn the corner, and they're gone.

I'll bet Red had no idea the pile of haunted antiques in his abandoned general store would someday bring a guy like me and a girl like Beth together, but it did. Part of me hopes the Markles will keep selling that creepy, old junk. That same part of me hopes that when another ghost turns up, Beth will call me again to help.

I smile. Part of me knows she will.

ROBERT THE DOLL

Are some dolls really haunted? When he was a boy in the early 1900s, artist Robert Eugene Otto received a doll named Robert. The doll, which wears a sailor uniform, always scared Otto. It was said to have destroyed other toys and knocked over furniture. As the doll was passed on, other owners claimed that Robert would move from room to room, and at night they could hear the doll laughing and talking. Robert is now kept at at a museum in Key West, Florida. Legend has it that the doll brings bad luck to any tourist who takes his photo without permission.

ABOUT THE AUTHOR

Thomas Kingsley Troupe was afraid of just about everything as a kid. Now a full-fledged adult, he's become fascinated by the creepy, the strange, and the unexplained. In his spare time, he investigates ghostly activity with the Twin Cities Paranormal Society. With his own ghost squad, he's stayed in a few haunted places, including the Stanley Hotel in Colorado and the Villisca Murder House in Iowa.

ABOUT THE ILLUSTRATOR

Rudy-Jan Faber lives and works in the beautiful town of Leeuwarden in the Netherlands. Whenever Rudy has some time to spare, he loves to lock himself up in his attic and paint with oils. After leaving his job as a concept artist at a gaming studio, Rudy took up his passion for book illustration. He loves it when he can make illustrations for super spooky stories . . . or for stories with pirates, or for super spooky stories with pirates.

GLOSSARY

churning — to move or swirl roughly

closure — getting a sense of resolution at the end of something

dejected — sad and depressed

grimace — a facial expression usually indicating a negative reaction to something

hypnotized — to be put in a sleeplike state or trance

paranormal — having to do with an unexplained event that has no scientific explanation

porcelain — a hard ceramic made by firing and glazing clay

prowler — a person who moves around quietly and secretly, often in order to steal something

skeptical — doubting that something is really true

FURTHER INVESTIGATION

1. Casey is afraid to go to the Spring Fever Dance, but once there, he's glad he did. Were you ever surprised by an event you weren't looking forward to?

2. Casey and Hai are freaked out by the doll staring out of Mrs. LaPierre's window. Discuss something that creeps you out.

3. The maker of the dolls, Mrs. Darling, regrets not spending more time with her daughter while she was alive. Do you have any regrets?

4. Beth and Liz weren't sure their parents would ever believe they'd sold haunted antiques from their store. Why? Have you ever had a secret you didn't tell because you thought it might be unbelievable?

5. Draw a picture of a haunted antique. Then make up a story behind the antique and share it with a friend. Use your imagination to add spooky details!

Uncover the mysteries of
HAUNTIQUES...

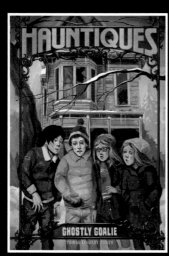

GHOSTLY GOALIE
THOMAS KINGSLEY TROUPE

PHANTOM'S FAVORITE
THOMAS KINGSLEY TROUPE

WANDERING WAGON
THOMAS KINGSLEY TROUPE

DARLING DOLL
THOMAS KINGSLEY TROUPE